MW00761055

The Shadow Soldier

By

Becca Boucher

The Shadow Soldier
Copyright Becca Boucher October 2015
All rights reserved.
Second Printing

Acknowledgement

This second edition would not be if it wasn't for the help of two amazing women. My writing partners, Chasity Conley and Jamie Sue Wilsoncroft. These two women are amazing authors in their own right, to work with them is a privilege.

Credit also goes out to my family members in the armed forces. Without your stories, technical advice, and all around knowledge, this story would not feel as real.

And finally my dad. Sitting on your knee, hearing stories, and being told I could be anything I wanted, started me on this great journey of writing. I hope there are books in heaven.

This book is dedicated to all the men and woman serving in the United States Military. May God bless you and your families.

"Rangers never die, they go to hell to regroup."~~ Army Ranger Moto

August 2012

"Tell me again why we're going to Hampton Beach?" Megan stared out the window of the Nissan Altima as it sped up 495 and away from Boston.

"Because it's 90 degrees at home. And I'm getting sick of the Southie guys pretending they're homies from the Jersey Shore." Megan sighed at her best friend's comparison, as Dee rolled her eyes and put her blinker on to change lanes.

"Did you seriously just say that? Like Hampton is going to be any better. It's going to be super crowded and full of drunk college guys."

The last thing Megan wanted to do was spend the weekend at Hampton Beach. Memories of ditching her high school boyfriend on the boardwalk mingled with pictures of her dad packing the station wagon sky high with plastic beach chairs. The last thing she wanted to do was spend another summer day with the crowds of humanity at Hampton. She would rather be home in Boston's Back Bay, painting on her small easel, on her equally small balcony. She wasn't an introvert or anything, she just preferred the quiet things in life. Unlike the boisterous Dee.

"Plus, you might just find a hot guy. It's been what, three months since you had a date?"

Dee's voice jarred Megan from her musings. "Try two. Who's keeping track anyway. I'm perfectly happy the way I am. A strong independent woman."

"You keep telling yourself that Megs." Dee patted her knee as she pulled off the highway.

***

Megan had long stopped trying to keep track of Dee in the crowd of people down by the water's edge. The Atlantic seemed to be colder here than anywhere she had been, she preferred her beach chair and umbrella to the thrashing waves. Let her friend have them.

Taking one last look before she went back to her book, she found her; Dee waved to her before she started chatting up some guy. Megan muttered to herself, weren't they too old for this? Suddenly she found herself propelled sideways out of her chair and across the sand. Adding more insult to injury, she was trapped under one big hunk of man.

"Excuse me! Can you get the hell off of me?" Megan scampered and pushed herself away as she yelled. Managing to turn herself around, she found the brightest blue eyes she had ever seen just inches from her face. They were attached to an equally impressive man, the guy was gorgeous. Not model gorgeous, but all muscle, tattoos, and crew cut hair. He just oozed sex appeal and strength. Suddenly she realized he was talking to her. His hand extended out to help her up.

"Oh man. Are you okay, ma'am'?" His southern accent made the 'ma'am' sound like molten lava. She shook her head to clear the fog, and reached for his outstretched hand. "The Frisbee got away from me, I had no clue I was gonna trip over that dog." He pulled her up and held on to her hand a little longer, waiting for her response. "Are you ok? My buddy Mitch has medic training, I can get him to take a look at you."

Her eyes focused in on the huge tattoo on the left side of his chest. A crest of some sort that had Army Ranger above it, and 'Death before dishonor' below it. He was military. That made sense.

"I'm... I'm fine. You just took me off guard. I apologize for yelling at you like that." She pushed the hair out of her eyes, and felt her hand shaking. "Wow, I guess I need a drink."

"Hey, come here." He took her hand again and led her over to her stuff. Righting her beach chair and pushing the umbrella back into the sand. "Sit, you took a big spill."

Megan did as she was told and sat down. Why she was following the orders of this stranger? She couldn't stop looking at him. He chuckled.

"My name's Bob. What's yours?"

"Megan. Megan Davenport."

"Well Megan Davenport, do you have anything to drink in that cooler there? You sure look like you could use some H2O. Crap did I just say H2O?" The last part was said more to himself than her, and she couldn't help but laugh.

"I think I have some juice." She watched the muscles in his back ripple as he reached over and grabbed a bottle of juice out of her cooler. What was she doing? She couldn't get obsessed over some random, hot, southern, soldier on the beach. Dee could, but not her. She reached out to take the juice from him and their fingers touched, like some damn clichéd movie. But he held her eyes, until someone started yelling his name.

"Bob! What the fuck, man? We're in the middle of something and you fall over and disappear."

"That's Mitch. Ummm I gotta go." He stood and smiled at her. His teeth just a little crooked, and started to turn around. "See ya." He waved, and jogged down the beach with one last look behind him.

***

It took all her will power not to tell Dee about the random hotness that was Bob. If she had, Dee would have been all over her for details, grilling her like a police detective. As she faked sleep on the way home, she thought of all the millions of ways the whole encounter could have gone better. She could have asked him to have a drink with her, asked him his last name, or gotten his number. God, she really was socially awkward. His face played behind her closed eye lids, she had no idea why, guys never affected her like this. Then she remembered she was leaving for Georgia and that conference tomorrow. That would take her mind off it.

***

The terminal at Logan was packed. Megan ran the last twenty feet to her gate, pulling her carry on behind her. Oversleeping, almost missing her cab, and getting stuck with the slowest TSA agent in Boston, all combined to make her one more mishap short of being a raging bitch. She grabbed her boarding pass back from the gate agent and made her way onto the plane. Finding the first aisle seat she could, she plopped down into it and closed her eyes. This conference better be worth it.

She was vaguely aware of the other passengers taking their seats and storing luggage. Focusing instead on relaxing for the takeoff, flying was one of her least favorite things. Suddenly she was jolted out of her thoughts by a soft southern drawl.

"Excuse me, ma'am. Can we squeeze by you? Those seem to be the last two seats on the plane."

Opening her eyes, Megan was met with the same startling blue eyes she had seen on the beach the day before. Only this time they topped one impressively dressed soldier sporting a tan beret.

"Oh, of course. Wow, it's you." Did she just say that out loud? But a look of recognition slowly dawned on Bob's face. His name *was* Bob, wasn't it?

"Megan Davenport, the girl I knocked over on the beach. How are ya, darling?" Was he playing the accent card?

"You remembered my name, impressive." She grinned like a school girl as she stood to let the two men pass. They settled into the seat, than he turned back to her.

"Megan, this is my friend Mitch. Mitch, this is Megan, and in case you forgot, I'm Bob."

"I didn't forget." She giggled nervously as Bob's huge smile beamed at her. Suddenly Mitch's hand was in her face.

"Nice to meet you, Megan. Sorry this big galoof ran you over yesterday. I guess he forgot all the manners his momma taught him." He settled himself into his seat as the captain began to speak over the intercom.

"Ladies and Gentlemen, welcome to flight 217 to Columbus Georgia, the skies are clear and we should be landing in about 3 hours and twenty minutes."

People started to buckle seatbelts and prepare for takeoff. Megan's hands shook nervously at the close proximity of Bob. The man had haunted her dreams all night, and now he sat next to her, gorgeous in his uniform, all muscles and southern drawl.

Why was it that just days after convincing herself she didn't need a man to be happy, this one kept falling into her lap? Literally. Wait. Was he talking to her again?

"So, why are you headed to Columbus?"

"Me? Ummmm … Work. A work conference on transition planning for young adults. I work in special education." She hoped to God she didn't sound as stupid as she felt.

"Wow that's awesome. I admire teachers, especially ones who work with such high risk kids. I've seen a lot of places where kids need that help, and they just don't get it."

She loved the sound of genuine admiration in his voice. And tried not to stumble on her words. "Why are you headed there?"

"It's our home base, 75th Ranger Regiment Fort Benning Georgia, at your service." Next to them Mitch rolled his eyes at Bob and placed ear buds in. It was obvious he wasn't in the mood for chatting. "Don't mind Mitch, he likes to hide the fact we're Special Forces." He gave Megan an exaggerated wink.

"Ummmm, maybe you shouldn't be telling me you're Special Forces?"

"Nah, it's not as taboo as you might think. I'll just have to kill you when we get off the plane."

She sucked in a breath as Bob doubled over in laughter at the look on her face. "I'm kidding, Megan. Seriously, as long as I don't tell you where we're headed, or our mission, it's all good. We just got off leave. Two weeks in New England with Mitch's family, I'm ready to head back to the Taliban." Mitch gave him the finger and Megan chuckled.

"You guys remind me of my brothers. Always fighting, from the like five minutes I've known you that much is evident. So you didn't like New England?"

"No, I loved it. Seriously, I am so thinking of retiring up here. Boston is amazing. I know it seems people do it the other way around, go down south, but I fell in love with Boston. Hell, since I saw Cheers re-runs as a kid I always wanted to go there."

It was Megan's turn to laugh. "Why is it everyone I meet from down south references Cheers to me?"

"You don't all 'pak the cah in the Havad Yawd'."

She doubled over at his hilarious attempt at a Boston accent. "No. Not so much." She was enjoying their obvious flirting.

"Where are you from?" Bob grew serious.

"Worcester. It's about forty eight miles west of Boston. I moved to Boston for college and never looked back. Worcester is great, but we're kind of like the laughing stock of the Commonwealth. Plus I'm working on my doctorate, the commute would be too much."

"Your Doctorate? No shit. That's amazing, Megan. Good for you. I'm in awe of people who can make it that far in school, who can accomplish so much."

Did he just say he was in awe of her? A Special Forces soldier in awe of a teacher?

"You're in awe of me? You blow stuff up and go after bad guys and you're in awe of me? I owe you a debt of gratitude."

Bob got quiet. His eyes focused on his hands as he twisted them in his lap. "It's just my job, ma'am. I get real uncomfortable with praise. There is nothing glorious about killing."

His voice grew so sad, Megan reached for his hand before she even realized what she was doing. He took it and clung to her like a life line. They sat that way for a while, quiet as the plane buzzed around them. Finally Megan spoke, she had to, the weight of his hand in hers tingled with emotion.

"Why did you join the military?"

He looked up at her and chuckled. That southern boy charm sparkling in his eyes. "No one ever asked me that before. Ten years ago I was looking for something, anything, after I graduated from high school. This recruiter came to my shop and asked who wanted money for college. I jumped without thinking. Next thing I know, I'm on my way to basic training." His thumb absentmindedly stroked the back of her hand as he spoke. Intimate and new, Megan never wanted him to let go. "I was supposed to be in motor pool, diesel trucks. Next thing I know, my drill sergeant comes to me and says I'm top of the class, Ranger material. Then, I'm graduating Ranger school and heading on my first mission. Three tours in Afghanistan later, I'm thinking there's nothing glorious about war. I'm sick of it."

The hesitation was back in his voice. "You're so easy to talk to Megan. I've never said that to anyone before."

He glanced at Mitch, who was sleeping, his ipod slipping from his hand. "Certainly not Mitch. He's my best friend in the world. Has my back, saved my ass countless times. I'm his unit commander. Shit like I just said, makes me sound weak." His eyes were back focused on the ground and he slipped his hand out of Megan's. She missed the warmth instantly.

"Don't say that." She placed her hand on his cheek and turned his face toward her. "From the little I know about you, I would never peg you as weak. What you've seen over there, I don't even want to know. I just know, there's goodness in your heart. I see it."

Without thinking Megan leaned over and pressed a kiss to his cheek. What was she doing? She had no time for this. A stranger on a plane. A stranger who unexpectedly keeps dropping into her life. There once was a time she would have taken that as a sign. But now, she had spent the last year proving to herself she could live life without being part of a couple.

Then Bob glanced at her, a cheeky smile on his face, and a glint of wetness in his eyes, and her heart was lost. Lost to the sexy soldier that kept sweeping her off her feet.

***

They talked for a good hour, until Megan fell asleep and her head rested on Bob's shoulder. Before he knew it, the flight was over. Much too soon for his liking. As he went to gently shake Megan as they approached for landing, he saw Mitch wink at him and laugh. Mitch was usually the pick-up artist, girls on every coast. Bob was the soulful one. The sleepy look in her eyes made his heart skip a beat, this girl had caught him hook, line, and sinker.

"Megan, I hate to tell you this, but we're landing."

She looked at him and sighed. "Already? God, I needed that nap."

"Umm, is it too forward to ask where you're staying at? I mean, how long are you in Columbus for?"

She blushed a little. Something he found very endearing.

"I'm only here till Wednesday, three days. And I'm afraid the conference is going to take up most of my time. But, I'm staying at the Double Tree here at the airport." She reached into her purse and pulled out a business card. "Here's my cell number, shoot me a text if you're ever up in Boston again."

Bob took the card and stuck it in his pocket. Was she blowing him off? They started to collect their carry-ons and make their way off the plane. At the end of the jet way Megan stopped and waited for them.

"Thank you, Bob, for making this flight so enjoyable. And I guess for running into me on the beach yesterday." She stood on her tiptoes to place a kiss on his cheek. Then turned to Mitch. "Nice to meet you too, Mitch." She winked at them both and turned to make her way through the terminal.

"And you just let her walk off." Mitch stuck an imaginary microphone in Bob's face. "How does it feel to connect with a total stranger, than let her give you the slip?"

"Shut up, Mitch. I got her number."

"You actually gonna call her? Or is it going to end up in your drawer with all those other numbers you collected and never called?"

"Fuck. You. Mitch. Is it fair to string these girls along and start something with them when we're off, to god knows where, nine months out of the year?"

"No one said anything about a relationship. When was the last time you got laid?"

Bob stormed off, his mind all in a jumble. Mitch was way over the line. He yelled back over his shoulder to him. "She's not that kind of girl, jackass."

***

Tuesday night dragged on and Megan was tired. The conference had been amazing, a ton of information in a few days.

But it had also been exhausting. As she entered her quiet hotel room it suddenly hit her, why she had been so distracted. A part of her had been waiting for Bob to call. She checked her cell phone. Nothing, just a text from Dee telling her she would pick her up at the airport the following evening.

Well, wasn't that what she wanted? She wasn't even sure she wanted a date. Never mind one with an Army Ranger. But, she realized a part of her was disappointed. She thought of the look in Bob's eyes as he told her his biggest secret. Maybe she imagined she had felt a connection.

Getting out of the shower, she heard the room phone ring and wrapped the robe a little tighter around herself. Who would be calling her here?

"Ms. Davenport? There is a delivery for you at the front desk. It's being requested you come down and get it."

Okay, this was a little weird. She looked out the window and calmed her nerves. If it was the hotel lobby, with people around, it should be okay. Right? "Of course. I need a few, but I will be down as soon as I get dressed."

The voice on the other end of the phone kind of chuckled. "No problem, ma'am. Take your time."

As soon as Megan entered the lobby, the first thing she saw was Bob standing there. Civilian clothes, and a red rose clutched in his hands. She stopped in her tracks and caught her breath. He was even more attractive than she remembered. A huge smile lit up her face.

"Good evening, Megan. Would you do me the honor of accompanying me to dinner?"

Her cheeks turned the most adorable shade of red, and Bob couldn't help himself. He took two steps closer, took her in his arms, and kissed her. When they broke apart, Megan chuckled. God, he loved that sound.

"I would love to go to dinner with you."

***

Bob was so easy to talk to. After they had eaten in a cozy little café, they had walked hand in hand along the Riverwalk. Something Megan would had never known was there. It was romantic, in an understated kind of way. They talked about everything from their childhoods and families, to career goals. They stood under the faint glow of a street light as Bob told her about the last mission he had been on in Afghanistan. They were headed back in three months to help train local police forces.

"The scary thing about Rangers, we don't just go in to fight back. We go looking for the enemy. There's no turning back when you're in the middle of some little hellhole Afghan town. Our backs are always against the wall. It makes you think." He grew quiet as they stood hand in hand watching boats float into the inlet. "I didn't mean for this to happen, Megan."

"For what to happen?" she was confused by his sudden change in topic.

"To be falling for someone I just met." The words rushed out of him like a fountain. "I have tried my hardest for the last ten years to not form any relationship other than with my brothers, my fellow Rangers. Guys like Mitch, they can sleep with a different girl at every duty station and be fine with it. Me, I have had two girlfriends the last decade, and I always felt like I was short changing them. But damn it, Megan. I can't get you out of my head."

Was she hearing him right? "Bob, I .... It's ok. We can take this slow." Her words were interrupted by his kiss. Soul searing and needy. He nibbled at her lips, wrapped his hand around the back of her neck and pulled her in deeper. It was intense, and when he pulled back, she felt like she had been claimed. Every word of reason she had vaporized at her lips.

"I'm sorry, Megan. I'm sorry, I hope I didn't cross a line."

"Kiss me again, Bob." She pulled him back to her.

***

Dinner turned into breakfast in bed. Megan couldn't remember the last time she had slept with someone on a whim.

But Bob felt like coming home. His arms felt like heaven as he wrapped her up next to him. She couldn't believe how fast the night had passed, and dreaded the fact she had to go home, and he had to report to base in an hour. How could they figure all this out in an hour? She leaned into him and sighed.

"I never would have figured you for a guy who likes to cuddle, a girl could get used to it."

Bob chuckled. "I never used to be."

"What changed?"

"I guess it's the person I'm with." As he said it he pressed little kisses to her back.

Megan felt her eyes get wet. Could he be any sweeter? "Bob, what are we going to do? How are we going to work this? What if we both leave this room and we never get this feeling again. Can this work?"

He turned her over and crawled on top of her. "I promise you, Megan Davenport, this will work. After this next deployment, I'm cycling out. I'm done. I had been thinking of it, but last night as I watched you sleep. I knew it. I fell into you on that beach for a reason, we were on that plane together for a reason. I used to think my life was the military, but my life is so much more. I can make a difference here. Look, I could be a Boston Police detective." Megan chuckled at the thought. "Wait for me, Megan. Give this a chance?"

She nodded. "I'll wait for you." A promise sealed by a kiss.

***

November 2012

"Are you scared?" Dee watched Megan as she cleaned up her small studio apartment, making room for Bob who was coming in later in the afternoon.

"Why the hell would I be scared? We have been texting, and talking, and skyping for three months. And I went down to

Savannah last month for his grandmother's funeral. It's not like we're just meeting the first time. Geeze."

The last three months had been crazy. She and Bob talked every day, if they had been in the same state, they would have been inseparable. She knew they were meant to be together like she knew they needed air to breath. She wanted to yell at anyone who tried to lecture her about love at first sight, and the dangers of falling too fast. Bob was a once in a life time kind of man. Sure she had seen his demons. Last month when they had been at his mom's, he had woken up in the night screaming. Night terrors and cold sweats had been plaguing him for a year. And there were times he would seem disconnected. She had begged him to see someone when he got back to base. But he had refused. He just wanted to make it to the first of the year, and this last mission. Then he would be out. She agreed, but it didn't mean she wasn't worried.

"No, I mean are you scared he's going back over there after this visit?" Dee snapped her out of her reverie with her question.

"I'd be stupid if I wasn't. He can't tell me much, but I know this tour is going to be his hardest. I'm worried that he already has some PTSD, I can't bear to lose him to his own demons. That would be worse than losing him over there."

"You really have it bad for him, Megan. I can see it."

"I love him, Dee. One day you wake up and it smacks you in the head. If you hadn't dragged me to Hampton last August, I never would have met him. Or felt this happy."

"He is hot! And that 'awe shucks' country boy drawl, damn girl. I wish he had fallen over me."

"Dee, go home." Megan gave her friend a good natured push toward the door. "I'll call you tomorrow."

"Fine. But see if soldier boy has a friend for me, will ya?" Dee winked as she left.

Megan closed the door on Dee and leaned up against it. How was she going to fit a year's worth of love into four days? Maybe she was a fool. But her heart wouldn't let her do anything different.

***

"The John Hancock Building." Bob rolled over in bed and nuzzled the back of Megan's neck. They had spent most of yesterday in bed, making love and talking. The day before they had hit every tourist attraction in town. From Fenway to the Freedom trail, she took him everywhere she could think of. Even the incredibly corny version of Cheers that resided in Faneuil Hall. Two days left.

"What about it?"

"I can see it from your window. But I want to go to the top of it. I want to see all of Boston before I leave." Bob kissed her lightly. "I want to feel the mist off the harbor blow into my face."

She giggled. "The observation deck isn't open air. But we can go."

He kissed her and jumped up from bed. "Awesome. Let's do it. Wait a second baby girl, there's something I want to give you." Bob jogged over to his suitcase and pulled a t-shirt and a teddy bear dressed in Ranger gear from it. "Something to hold onto while I'm gone."

She took the t-shirt and pressed it to her face. It smelled of him. All musky and woodsy, instant tears came to her eyes. "This is so much harder that I thought it would be."

"Me too, baby. But we will get through it. I love you more than there are stars in the sky. And just think, those same stars I sleep under, they're the ones you'll be sleeping under."

"That's so corny, Bob." Megan laughed. "But at the same time so beautiful. I love you too. Nothing will ever change that. Nothing." She jumped out of bed. "Wait, I have something for you too." She ran over to her dresser and grabbed the small plastic case she had got in the mail just days before. "I had a key chain made for you." She tossed him the case. "We can take a picture at the Hancock and put it in there."

Bob pulled the key chain out, one side was blank to slide a picture in, the other side held one of those silly pre-printed sayings. But this one made sense. He loved it as he read it out loud. "Keep calm, I'm a Ranger." He held it to his heart. "It's perfect, baby girl. Just like us."

October 2013

Megan threw her cell phone across the room and watched it slide down the opposite wall, just as she slid down the wall she was leaning on. Her phone survived, encased in its unbreakable shell. But she wouldn't. As soon as she hit the floor her head fell into her hands and between her knees. Her fingers tore out her hair, her stomach wretched, and a primal cry escaped her lips. She was blinded by tears, choked by sobs. Why couldn't the walls cave down on her? She would just sit here and wait. Wait for her heart to stop beating. Wait for another call to say it was all a joke. Wait for someone to tell her Bob was still alive.

Four Days Earlier

The bell alerting Megan to a new Skype call had dinged on her computer and she wasted no time in running over to it. She flipped up the screen delighted to see Bob. "Hey, Babe!" He was sitting in his barracks, the stark beige wall behind him peppered with pictures, post cards, and flags. He looked tired, but still handsome. The dessert camouflage made his eyes look even more strikingly blue. His hair was shaggy though, almost touching his eyes. After all these months he still looked so hot. The sight of him made her stomach turn loops and summersaults.

"Sexy man, how are you?!" The glee was evident in her voice and it made Bob smile. He had been afraid this last deployment would be the end of them. Sure he had been active duty when they met, but he had been gone most of their relationship. He was so excited to tell her this was it. He was coming home state side to stay. As soon as they went out on this last recon he was all hers. He laughed.

"Listen, Babe. We are heading into the mountains for the next three days. No contact for a while, but I got great news."

Megan's stomach felt sick at hearing him say they were heading out again. The last time something bad had happened. All he had been able to tell her was they were almost ambushed, but some local rebels had come to their aide. She knew winter was setting into the Afghan mountains, he would have the weather as well as the enemy to contend with. "Really, Babe? What's that?" She tried hard to hide her bad feeling.

"Don't look so worried, Megan." She laughed a little at his comment, and decided she needed to work on her poker face. "It's good news. After this recon my unit is coming home. Then I'm done. Finished. I'll be all yours, baby. All yours!" He pumped his fist with a little woop-woop.

"For real? Bob, honey, are you sure this is what you want? I mean don't let me stand in the way of your dreams." She felt guilty that as she said the words, her heart was fluttering with excitement. Bob would be home for good. No more sleepless nights. She could finally allow herself to love him with all her heart and not have to worry.

"Megan, this is what I want. I accomplished everything I set out to do when I signed up for this crazy ride. The Army Rangers are not my whole life. You need to be my life. Ten years is long enough."

Trying as hard as she could to stop them, the tears still cascaded down her face. "Bob. I love you, honey. This is amazing news." She reached out and placed her hand against the screen, and he did the same. Their hands perfectly lining up, finger to finger.

"Megan, sweetie, open your eyes." She hadn't realized she had closed them, or how long she had sat like that. It was almost as if she could feel him, even though he was thousands of miles away. "Babe, I have to go. We have a briefing in a few about this mission. Please try not to worry. It should be easy in easy out, like a walk in the park." She nodded and tried to convey every feeling she had for him through the computer screen. It felt like years since they had been together last, the shirt he had left her with his favorite cologne was starting to lose its smell, and she couldn't bear it.

"Okay, Hun. Just please be careful. Don't try and be a hero, leave that to Mitch."

He laughed so hard she thought he might fall over. God, it wasn't that funny. Just then people started to walk behind him in the barracks, activity picking up. "Listen, Megan. I have to go. But promise me you won't worry. And oh yah, watch the mail, babe. I sent something out last week and it should be there soon. A very special package." He winked and wagged his eyebrows at her. "Promise me you won't open it until we can open it together ok?"

"Bob, what the hell kind of package is that? I have to wait till you get home? Are you trying to kill me?"

He laughed again, this time not as long and loud. More people came into the room, and then Mitch stood behind him and made rude gestures behind his head. Totally ruining the moment. Suddenly a gruff voice from the distance said something Megan couldn't make out. But it sounded serious.

"You better go, Hun. Call me as soon as you can to let me know when you'll be back on US soil."

Bob nodded. "Try not to worry, Babe. I love you. Two beers and a coke." With that the screen went black. And a feeling of dread hit her like a thousand bricks dropped from the Empire State building. She just felt off and she couldn't put her finger on it. Standing up from her desk she walked across the room and grabbed the old army t-shirt off her bed and pressed it to her nose. Bob's woodsy sent still held on. It comforted her. But soon it wouldn't be enough.

Three Days Earlier

"Arizona, Bunker Hill and Majestic, your pickup point will be on the other side of this mountain ridge. The window is small. But, with the mission as it stands. You should have no issues meeting your deadline." Bob sat in the stark briefing room with his team trying to take in the mission parameters. "This is an easy one guys. We get in, plant the communication device, grab the girl, and get the hell out. It's imperative we get this girl out of the hands of the Taliban. She has information that could lead us to public enemy number two. And she is in need of political asylum, her stand on education is not well received in this village."

All around him guys were taking notes and joking. But his mind was on Megan, and the nagging feeling he had in the pit of his stomach. For everything his commanding officer was saying, he didn't believe this one was as easy as it sounded. He had been having dreams about the shadow soldier for the last few days. He would wake up in cold sweats, screaming for the guy to duck for cover. But the soldier in his dream kept advancing into enemy fire, being pelted with bullets and RPGs, never stopping, just walking forward. Shit, he had even thought he had seen him on patrol the other night. The NATO guys thought he was losing it when he yelled for him to get back to point. And there was no one off their post. Fuck, the sooner he got out of Kabul the better.

He tried talking to Mitch about the shadow soldier. "Hey, have you ever seen someone out in the field? Like this random soldier who is just walking around lost."

Mitch dropped his fork and looked at Bob like he had six heads. "Like a mirage? Or like some grunt gone AWOL?"

"No, just like a random, I don't know, almost like a ghost. Like one that comes up before we have a scrimmage, or before we feel out some insurgents. It's like he's leading me through the fire, but, sometimes I think he's leading me to hell."

Mitch stared at him with his mouth open and little bits of hamburger bun lodged in his scruffy beard. The look in his eyes was one of mirth. "Fuck, Bob. Are you forgetting to put your hat on in the sun? Winter is blowing in but shit the desert sun still gets bright. You might be frying your brain." He reached over and smacked Bob off the side of the head. "Seriously, Bob, keep that shit to yourself. If you start talking about ghosts, or walking zombie soldiers, they will put you in the back room and take away your weapon. God damn."

Mitch picked his fork back up and looked back to his plate.

Bob grunted. "Fuck you, Mitch. I'm serious. You don't remember that old timer back in Fort Dix who told stories about the shadow soldier? And how he visited when you were going to lose one of your guys. He said he saw him at Normandy, and at one other place I can't remember where, but guys have seen him in battle."

"Normandy? Really, Bob? That old timer was messing with you. Hell, by the time his platoon hit the beach it was a blood bath. He probably saw some guy walking around in shock all bloody, and eighty years later he's calling it a ghost. Bob, seriously. You've been on tour after tour, you have a new girlfriend back at home. It's just the stress getting to you. You need a change of scenery, man."

The voice of his mission commander snapped him back to the present. "Alpha Group, you have point for this one. When the chopper drops you off, you have an hour to get in, plant the device and grab Delbar. Get her back to the chopper. Icing is a real concern up there right now. We can't have the chopper on the ground that long. You three are the backbone of this mission. Bob is your point man, code name Bunker Hill. You got it?"

Bob groaned internally. Fuck. Not only was this mission giving him the heebee geebies, he was point man. Mitch slapped him on the back. "Hell of a way to go out, man. When we pull this off, Newsweek will hail us as humanitarians for getting this girl out. Better tell that shadow soldier to take a back seat." Mitch laughed so hard the commander gave them a dirty look. Bob let his head hit the desk before he gave Mitch a look that could freeze hell.

Later that night Bob laid awake and stared at the ceiling above his bunk. His mind raced. Images of Megan. Of Mitch back in Ranger training. Of the last few missions they had gone out on. Images of insurgents and Taliban fighters. They all assaulted him. But he was always able to come back to Megan's smiling face. The last time they made love in her small apartment overlooking Boston's Back Bay, and the way they had laid for hours after. Never moving, just talking about all they wanted. That was when he decided for sure he was not re-upping when his time was up this June. He hadn't told her then, he wasn't sure it was a possibility. But when all the cards fell into place, he picked the ring up from some street vender in Kabul. A blue onyx that reminded him of the sky over the harbor that day in her bed. After the second time he saw the shadow soldier, he got nervous. He boxed up the ring and mailed it out to her last week.

Suddenly he was standing out in front of the barracks. His gun was slung across his shoulders, and his boots were not even tied. He could see over the wall and out to the desert, across air field and vast emptiness, to where he knew lights should be in the distance. And someone was calling to him. As plain as day his name was being said from the other side of the wall. Whispered, yet he heard it. Through the pitch black darkness he followed the sound. His footsteps not even making noise on the gravel. Then the man was in front of him. The shadow soldier. Dressed in fatigues that were slightly outdated but certainly American. Bob raised his hand in greeting, the man raised his gun and fired.

Bob sat bolt upright in bed, his face flushed with sweat and his pulse racing. Had he called out in his nightmare? Looking around his bunk he saw Mitch and Coop sound asleep. "Shit, that was close." His whisper sounded loud and foreign to his own ears. Running his hands through his hair he tried to calm himself some. "It was a dream. Wasn't it?" Looking down he realized his boots were on, and they were muddy.

***

It was shortly after five and Megan was making her way from the bus stop across busy Huntington Ave. Her goal was singular, coffee and a scone from Temptations Café, and then, a warm bath and bed in her cozy brownstone apartment. Her day had been crazy, to say the least. If one more parent had come for a late pickup she would have blown her top. And the cold she had been fighting was starting to take her down.

She entered the café, nodding to the young couple from her building who sat in the window seat, and quickly made her way to the counter. She had no patience for small talk. But crap, Phyllis was behind the counter. She could never get away from her. Hopefully she looked sick enough the kind older woman would just give her the usual and let her be on her way.

"Megan! Come here let me see you. Are you all right, dear?" Yah, no such luck.

"Actually, Phyllis, I think I'm coming down with whatever is going around. I'm just looking forward to getting home." The older woman took her in with worried eyes and started making up her order. "The usual, dear?"

"That would be better than perfect, Phyllis." Megan hoped her warm smile was genuine enough.

"How's Bob? Have you heard from him?" At the mention of Bob's name, Megan's eyes started tearing up and a lump unexpectedly formed in her throat. She had been unable to shake this worried feeling she had been having all day. Like something horrible was going to happen to Bob.

"Oh dear, I'm so sorry." Phyllis must have noticed her shiver.

"Oh no, it's nothing like that, Phyllis. I'm just missing him something bad today. Must be because I don't feel so good."

"Thank God. Why don't you go home and get some rest, dear?"

Megan turned for the door speaking over her shoulder as she did. "That's my plan, Phyllis. Thanks so much. See you later." As the door to the café slid closed behind her, she took a deep breath. Tasting the salt in the air, and hearing the rush of the city noise in her ears, calmed her.

Digging in her purse for her keys and juggling her coffee as she walked up the front steps of her brownstone, Megan almost missed the rumpled guy sitting by the door. His presence made her jump, he seemed to come out of nowhere and looked like he hadn't slept in days. He was dressed in old military style fatigues, but nothing like she had ever seen Bob in. He looked intently at her until she spoke.

"Can I help you, sir? Are you looking for someone?"

"No one in particular, ma'am. I just heard a soldier lived here and thought he might be able to help out an old grunt. I haven't had a warm meal in days."

Megan was a little suspicious. Downtown you could find a number of places to help out. Soup kitchens and shelters. The man was starting to make her nervous. There was no way in hell she was telling him Bob wasn't around.

"Well, sir, I think you have the wrong apartment building. But I can give you a few dollars to help you out." She wanted the man off her steps. He was looking too intently at her, and she was thankful her upstairs neighbor had just parked his car.

"No, I couldn't take your money ma'am. Just wanted to check things out." His words made her shiver.

Turning her attention to the door, Megan nodded her head. "Okay then. I hope you find what you're looking for." When she turned back to see if he left, she almost dropped her things. It was like he faded away in front of her eyes. Drifting like vapor down the steps and totally disappearing. She shook. She must be sicker than she thought if she was hallucinating old soldiers on her door step. She choked back the feeling of dread she had been having and made her way up to her apartment. Locking the extra deadbolt for the first time in months.

***

Two Days Earlier

Bob sat in the back of the Blackhawk as it made its way out of Kabul and toward the Pamir Mountains. Last night the dream, at least he thought it was a dream, about the shadow soldier was bad enough. But during the day today as they got ready for their mission, he had popped up all over the place. Everywhere he went the wisp of cold air followed, and the soldier would appear. He would just stare at him, his eyes intent and knowing. He nudged extra ammo toward him, and pointed out things Bob would otherwise have missed. Most disconcerting of all was the smell of Megan's lavender perfume. It seemed to follow him and envelop him, out of nowhere. Bob knew he was imagining it, there was no way Megan's fragrance could still be on some of his t-shirts.

Then the soldier spoke. "Watch your back, Bob. Sometimes the threats are from within." He jumped and spun around, thinking for sure Mitch was messing with him. But it was just the shadow, transparent and vague, lurking in the corner of the room. The sooner this mission was over, the better.

Mitch's voice from across the helicopter caught his attention. He cupped his hand around his ear to tell him he couldn't hear him over the deafening drone of the chopper's massive blades. So Mitch jumped across the gap and planted himself right next to Bob.

"Fuck dude, you look like you didn't sleep at all last night. Did the damn shadow soldier keep you up?" He wagged his eyebrows in mockery.

Bob groaned. "Shut the hell up, Mitch."

Mitch sat back and looked hard at Bob. Something was wrong. It might have been the way he didn't look directly at him when he talked, or the lack of humor in his response. Mitch had known Bob since Ranger school, the two had been through more recons together than you could count on two hands, and Mitch didn't like the fear in his eyes.

"I'm sorry, man. You okay? You just look really tired." Mitch looked at the other three guys and knew they were lost in their own worlds. IPod and magazines were passed around the bird, everyone trying to decompress before they landed.

Bob shook his head. "Ever get a feeling of foreboding, Mitch? Like something just isn't right? Something isn't sitting right with me and this mission. I just want it done and to start my cycle out." He looked intently at Mitch, gaging his reaction before he went on. "I know you think the shadow soldier is some kind of fairy tale, but it seriously has me freaked the fuck out. I mailed the ring to Megan last week. Just in case something happened to me. I think I'm losing my edge, Mitch."

"Fuck, Bob! That's the last thing I want to hear from our mission commander ten minutes before we drop into the middle of goddamned Taliban country. Get the fuckin shadow soldier out of your damn head. You are the best Ranger I know." Mitch turned and grabbed him on both sides of the head, forcing Bob to look him in the eyes. "You will complete this mission, and give Megan that ring again in person. I will make goddamned sure of it. You're tired. We both have been at this shit far too long, we need to get the hell out of this shit hole and back on US soil. And the fastest way to do it is get this girl out of the hands of the Taliban and bring her back with us. No half-baked ghost story should determine your future. You got that?" When Bob only nodded and smiled Mitch shook him by the shoulders and yelled it again in his face. "Do you fuckin get that?"

"I get it loud and clear, Sergeant!" And Bob did. Something in his mind took over and allowed him to focus on the mission. The shadow soldier forgotten. Mitch was right. He owed it to his guys to lead this outing with a clear head. He stood up and faced his guys, checking his watch.

"Six minutes until we drop into hell's kitchen, men. Mitch and I have point and will lead the rest of you into the compound. Just like we went over back at base. Stay in the shadows. Coop, you plant the tracker outside the North wall, it will pick up all enemy coms for a 1500 foot radius. Blake and Roger, you get us in the front door, we hold them back, grab our objective and haul ass back to the drop point. Easy in. Easy out. Two beers and a coke. Suit up, men."

As they turned to prepare for drop, Mitch grabbed Bob by the arm. "Why the fuck do you always say two beers and a coke?"

Bob laughed. "I have no fucking clue, man. My dad always said it every day after work, and on weekends before we went anywhere, he had to have two beers and a coke. I just say it. It's kind of my catch phrase."

"Your catch phrase? Since when do we have fuckin catch phrases?"

Bob glared at Mitch. "Since now. What do you want yours to be?"

"Shut the fuck up!"

Bob slapped him on the shoulder. "Well, shut the fuck up and get ready to drop." They both turned for the door of the chopper and bumped their fists together in silent salute. The cold Afghan mountains spread out below them like menacing sentries in the dark night.

***

About the time Bob and his team hit the snow covered Afghan ground, Megan sat bolt upright in bed. She was shaking, not from a fever, though that had certainly been the case a few hours before, but from a dream. In her dream, Bob was lost from the rest of his unit and trying to find his way back. He was cold and scared, and crying out for Megan. Her own face was wet with tears and she wiped them with the hem of her sheet. She hated this. She wanted to hold him, feel his heartbeat, and taste his kisses. She couldn't shake the feeling she never would see him again and it terrified her.

Making her way out of bed and to her small bathroom, she turned on the tap and splashed water on her face, cupping her hands and drinking some of it in. She breathed deep and tried to calm herself. Dreams were opposite. Her grandmother always told her that. It was just being sick that had her usually positive mind all kinds of mixed up. Yah that was it. When she woke up in the morning she would feel ten times better.

Crawling back in her bed she reached for Bob's old army shirt, her constant source of comfort these days. Pressing it to her face brought fresh tears to her eyes. It was losing its smell.

Outside a shadow lurked across the street under a street lamp. His hollow eyes were trained on Megan's window.

***

The snow cover wasn't really a surprise. They had flown into it as they made their way over the mountains. Bob led the small group of men over the traitorous ridge and down a steep embankment. From this vantage point they could see the compound. Weak lights illuminating small windows some ten

29

feet off the ground. He pointed to Coop and then to the far side of the compound wall. Coop nodded and made his way the forty feet across to slink up the wall. Bob checked his watch, it was 0300 hours. They had forty minutes to get in, grab the girl, and get back to the pickup point.

When Coop silently signaled with a quick burst of light that they were good, Bob motioned for the rest of the men to follow him. As they breached the compound wall, Bob detected some movement in one of the windows. Had they been spotted? Bob shook his head, no time for second glances now. They crawled up to the door and Blake and Roger pressed the plastic explosives into place, dragging the line back to the tree they spotted. In a matter of second the door blew off its hinges and the two men stormed into the building shouting commands in Uzbeki. Freighted woman and children crawled back into the shadows, as men defended their position.

Blake held off a group of men at gunpoint, forcing them to the ground as Roger motioned the rest of the team in. Bob and Mitch looked around the room, it was hard to tell which girl was the one they were looking for. And the men were hurling insults at them and spitting. Glancing at his watch, Bob realized they had twenty minutes left. It was make or break time. That's when he noticed movement to his right. The shadow soldier was standing in the corner of the stark room, his arms frantically motioning to Bob. None of the other guys seemed to notice him, in fact, they were intent on getting their point across to the men they held on the ground. He heard Mitch yelling at one of them to stay down, he vaguely heard the click of a gun.

Then he saw the girl. In the room behind the shadow soldier a young girl was tied to a chair. Her burka torn and disheveled, she looked at him with haunting eyes. Without further thought, or without motioning for one of his team to cover him, Bob stormed the room. As he reached the girl, he noticed the man standing behind her, laughing as he raised a late model soviet gun. Bob reacted and fired, hitting the man squarely in the chest. But not before the man had got off his own round, which hit Bob in the shoulder. The young girl screamed, but with all the shouting going on in the other room, no one heard her.

Bob stumbled back, momentarily shocked by the hit, but his adrenaline took over and he went to work trying to free the girl from her chair. "Shhh. It's ok. I'm American, we're going to take you away from here." He spoke in his broken Uzbeki, trying to calm the girl. Her eyes widened and she nodded. "Are you Delbar?" She nodded again and reached her hand out to touch his bleeding shoulder. He met her eyes. "It's ok, I've had worse." He was speaking in English now and she nodded again.

"He would have killed us both." Her eyes trained to the man bleeding out on the floor next to her.

"You speak English?"

"Why do you think I am such a threat to the Taliban? I refuse their advances, refuse to be their concubine. I help the American soldiers find the passage through the mountains. The man in the shadow, he told me you would come to get me."

Bob's breath hitched. "The man in the shadow?"

"Yes. He looked American, but spoke very much like me. We have to move."

Bob suddenly heard a commotion from the other room. His men were getting agitated, and the woman were begging them to leave. Glancing at his watch he noticed they had a little under fifteen minutes to pick up. He grabbed Delbar by the arm and pulled her toward the door just as his men opened fire. Two insurgents dropped to the ground and another put his arms up in surrender. Mitch yelled, "Where the fuck is Bob? We need to get out of here!" Blake motioned behind him and Mitch turned to meet Bob's eyes. "Shit man, he's hit!"

"Don't worry about me, move out! I'm right behind you." Blake looked at Delbar clinging to Bob's arm and nodded.

"He has the girl! Let's get the hell out of Dodge!"

The five of them made for the door, as they crossed the threshold they were met by blinding snow. The short time they had been in the compound was enough for the weather to change, it meant the rendezvous time would be even tighter. If the chopper was on the ground too long, the blades would ice up.

Mitch pushed Bob and Delbar through the door first, but she stumbled on the icy snow with her bare feet. As Bob reached down to pick her up, the voices from the house grew more agitated, and the remaining insurgent charged them.

All hell broke loose. Gunfire shot over their heads and Bob dived on Delbar to protect her. Just as he hit the ground, he felt piercing fire like pain rip through his lower back. They rolled over in the snow, and all he could register was the color red, goopy and warm, soaking the ground around him.

Mitch turned and shot the man point blank. The man's blood spraying him in the face, momentarily blinding him. He could make out the cries of the woman in the house, and yelled for them to get inside. As he wiped the warm blood from his face, he heard the frantic voice of Coop behind him.

"Fuck! Oh man! Fuck. Bob was hit again, and this time he's down."

Mitch grabbed the radio pinned to his shoulder and spoke franticly into it.

"This is Arizona, Bunker Hill, Majestic. We have taken enemy fire and have a man down. Repeat, we have a goddamned man down!"

Blake had grabbed Bob from the blood soaked snow and thrown him over his shoulder. Mitch made sure Delbar was attached to him, and pointed for the tree line where they were dropped. The Blackhawk was barley in sight through the blinding snow.

"Get the hell to the bird now."

He was aware of the girl's cries as they ran. But he resented them. Because of her they probably just lost Bob. As he pulled her over the boulders and icy rocks, he saw the trail of blood Bob's broken body was leaving. It made him wretch. He stumbled and lost hold of the girl, the snow had him all turned around. Looking up he saw no sign of anyone. Where was he? Where were his men?

Then he saw him. The dark figure loomed in front of him, lifting him up and pushing him toward the chopper. Mitch tried to speak to him, but the man just kept pushing him. Halfway up the hill he caught back up with everyone, just as Blake was handing Bob into the chopper. He fell into the chopper and took stock of his guys. Blake was franticly trying to stop the bleeding from Bob's back, but Bob was unresponsive and clear fluid drained from his nose. Spinal fluid? Mitch didn't want to think about it. Roger and Coop were trying to calm the girl down, but she was speaking rapidly, mixing Uzbeki and English and pointing out the door of the chopper.

All five men accounted for, Mitch signaled the pilot to take off. "Coop, who was that guy helping us up the mountain? Was he a local?"

Coop looked at Mitch like he was nuts. "What guy? We stumbled across the girl and you were nowhere to be seen for like five minutes. She said you let go of her and she lost you. And she's over here babbling about another soldier back in the house. Fuckin lost me."

Mitch rubbed his eyes. Now was he seeing shit too? He jumped across the aisle and ran back to check on Bob. This mystery guy would have to wait. "How is he, Blake?"

Blake looked at Mitch with tears in his eyes. "Not good man. We need to be back to base yesterday. He took a direct hit to the spinal column. I don't think he's going to make it."

"Oh shit, man." Mitch leaned down next to Bob's head. His breathing was almost nonexistent. His eyes glassy and lost. "Bob, man. You have to hang on. For Megan. I promised you man you would make it back to Megan." He took Bob's hand and held it in his own. But from the cold skin, and the slack feel, Mitch knew he was as good as gone. And the chopper hadn't taken off yet.

"Why the fuck is this bird not in the air? Get us in the goddamned air now!" Mitch yelled franticly and squeezed Bob's hand harder as the frozen blades of the Blackhawk finally started to spin.

***

Sometime just before dawn Megan sat bolt upright in bed. She couldn't shake the feeling that something was wrong. In fact, she felt like a part of her had just died. Bob's shirt was wrapped up in her arms and it quickly became damp from the tears cascading down her face. She got out of bed and made her way to her windows, she could just barely make out the sea port and the pink glow creeping into the morning sky. Some part of her deep down inside felt like this was an important day. One where her life would change. And she didn't feel like the change was good.

One Day Before

0700 hours the Blackhawk landed back at base in Kabul. By that time Bob's body had been covered, and Delbar had fallen asleep next to Coop. The turbulent flight back and the outcome of the mission weighed heavily on all the men. Mitch especially. He felt bad for ribbing Bob about the shadow soldier, and even worse for not covering him adequately. If he had just took out that last insurgent, Bob would still be here. And who the fuck was going to be the one to tell Megan. Not being married, she wasn't entitled to all the resources a wife would have gotten. Mitch had to call her. He felt like it was his duty.

Their rescue of Delbar was celebrated, and she was handed over to the UN very tearfully. Coop had taken a liking to her and was trying to figure out how to keep track of her whereabouts. But the loss of Bob was the main focus, their team had taken a heavy hit, and no one felt it more than Mitch. He spent the whole night with the Chaplin, his promise of getting Bob back to Megan weighed heavily on his mind. And he felt like the blame was squarely on his shoulders.

Just before day break he stood outside, a cold untouched cup of coffee in his hands, watching the sky lighten over the concreate barriers and barbed wire that separated the base from the desert expanse around Kabul. Then he saw it. A dark figure just past the barriers, his uniform was tattered and looked like it was from the last Gulf War. He raised his hand to wave, and Mitch raised his back in salute. Was he American? In what seemed like seconds, the man was closer. His face now clear to

Mitch. Weathered and tired it looked like the kind of face a kindly old uncle would have. And it was clearly American. Now even closer he could make out the name tag on the man's uniform. Clark. Hmmm, Mitch had no recollection of a Clark ever being on base. What the hell was going on?

Mitch motioned him closer to the chain link expanse and spoke. "Buddy, what are doing out there? Can we help you with anything?" Was he fading? It was getting harder to see the man. Maybe the noon day sun was playing tricks on him. Mitch tossed his coffee cup aside and dug the heels of his hands into his eyes.

When Mitch looked back up, the man nodded and stuck something toward him through the gap in the fence. "Your guy left this behind in the snow last night, he wanted to make sure you got it. He says to tell you that he's fine."

Mitch held his hand out and the plastic key chain dropped into it. He glanced at it and saw it said 'Keep calm, I'm a Ranger.' And recognized it immediately as the one Bob kept on him at all times, a gift from Heather. "Hey, Clark, or whoever you are, that shits not funny. My guy is far from fine! Where did you get this?"

The man didn't answer. He turned his back to Mitch and started walking away.

"Hey, asshole! I'm talking to you!" But before Mitch even had the words out of his mouth, the man had seemingly disappeared. A dark shadow floating like vapor in the desert sun replaced him.

Mitch turned the key chain over in his hands to see the scuffed picture on the other side. Bob and Megan posing for a selfie on the top of the John Hancock building. "Oh fuck, Bob! No! What the fuck is this!" Mitch sank to his knees and sobbed. "I'm sorry, Bob. I'm so goddamned sorry! Why did you have to send him? Why couldn't you fuckin come yourself? I didn't mean to fail you, Bob."

That Morning

The phone woke Megan up from such a deep sleep she couldn't even fathom what day it was. Rubbing her eyes, she glanced at the clock to see it was four in the morning. This better be good. "Hello?" Her sleepy voice instantly made the caller on the other end of the line wince in pain.

"Megan? Megan Davenport?"

"Yes, this is she. Who's calling?"

"Megan, its Mitch Crowley, Bob's friend. I need to talk to you."

The delay on the line made his words sound even more urgent. Megan snapped to attention.

"Oh God." Tears filled her eyes as the feeling of dread she had been having since yesterday came smacking back down on her. "Oh God no. Mitch, what happened?"

Mitch's voice broke. "Megan, it was supposed to be a routine mission, we were almost out of there. I'm sorry. I'm so very sorry."

"Is he okay, Mitch? Tell me he's ok, Mitch!"

The long gap of silence was telling.

"He's gone, Megan. I'm so sorry. He's gone."

***

Sometime later she woke up. Sunlight streamed through the windows over her bed like an unwelcome friend. Chunks of her hair laid at her feet, her cell phone rested across the room on the floor. Her throat hurt from screaming, the neighbors who came up to see if she was being attacked had left her with glasses of water and kind words. Kind words that rang hollow in her heart. She felt like a zombie.

She knew she should be doing something. Calling someone. But she couldn't even think clearly. Bob's mom surely had to know. She had met the kindly woman once last summer, when they had all gone down to Georgia for his grandmother's funeral. Megan guessed he would be buried there. Or maybe

Arlington? How did that work anyway? She crawled over to her phone to see she had three missed calls. Two were from Bob's mother, another one from Mitch. Or she guessed it was Mitch, it was the same oversees number that had called earlier. She sucked in a breath. She couldn't do it right now. She would have to call them later. Climbing back into bed with Bob's picture, she pulled the blankets over her head to hide from the world.

The banging on the door woke her up. Her head was killing her. Looking at the clock, she realized she had gone twenty six hours without eating. And she didn't know how many hours of those were spent hiding in her bed. The room was dark now, and whoever was at the door wasn't going away. She couldn't help but wonder who let them in the building. Shit. It had to be one of the neighbors checking on her again. She made her way out of bed and across the open expanse of her apartment. Looking through the peep hole she saw it was Pete from down the hall. She slowly opened the door.

"Hey, Megan. I'm sorry to bother you, but this guy was hanging around the building all afternoon. He looked like someone from the homeless veterans shelter, said his name was Clark? Anyway, he made me promise to give you this package. The damn thing had been sitting in your mail box since yesterday and it had him all worried. The guy barely said three words and then, took off."

Megan stared at him blankly looking at the small package in his hands. "You okay, Megan? Really, we could have called someone for you."

She shook her head. "Yah, I'm ok Pete. I just, Bob had said he was mailing a package. I forgot about it. With everything. Crap." Tears started to well up in her eyes.

"I'm sorry, Megan." Pete reached out to her, and she let him hug her for a second. But than her mind remembered something from the other day.

"Pete, that guy, did he look lost and confused? The other afternoon when I came home a strange guy was here. Looking for

Bob. Said he was told he could help him. It kind of made me uneasy. Then he just like, disappeared."

Pete shook his head knowingly. "Yah, like faded away. Or ran off quick. Know what, if he comes around again let me know. I don't like it. We don't need anyone hanging around. Don't go out alone, get me or Nancy to go with you. Especially at night."

Megan nodded her head. "Thanks, Pete." She was tired, even the light package in her hands was too much for her to bare. Backing into her apartment she nodded and quietly closed the door. Leaving Pete to wipe a tear of his own from his eye.

Two Weeks Later

The package sat on her table. Unopened. She had looked at it every day. Carried it in her suitcase to, and from, Bob's funeral. Never did anything with it, but hold it close to her heart. She stood quietly behind his mom at his funeral. Watched his team carry his casket. Accepted everyone's condolences like an actor going through all the motions. And missed him more.

And he was there. The strange man who kept appearing. Mitch took her by the elbow after the service at the cemetery and pointed to the tree line. There he stood, obscured by the shadows, a lost soldier watching them, fading in the noon sunshine. Was he the same creepy guy that showed up at her apartment? Couldn't be. And why did no one else acknowledge him?

Later after the service, Mitch took her aside and told her about Bob's visions of the shadow soldier. She stood and listened to him quietly, never saying a word. All the time tears welled in her eyes. Should she tell him she saw him too? Mitch was struggling, and Megan knew he needed something from her in the way of forgiveness, she just couldn't give it to him yet.

So here she sat, holding the package in her hands finally preparing to open it. It felt all wrong, Bob should be here to open it with her. Slipping her nail under the tape, she slowly started to pull it apart. Hitching her breath, wiping at her eyes, she worked it free until the box sat facing her, its flaps pulled down and its contents beckoning her. On top sat a blue piece of paper folded with her name written on it, in Bob's signature messy handwriting. She laughed a little, a noise she hadn't made in weeks. Picking it up revealed the small, black velvet box underneath. Oh shit. That couldn't be what she thought it was. Fresh tears prickled at the corners of her eyes. She decided it was better to ignore the jewelry box for now and read the letter. Picking it up, she held it lightly in her hands and opened the paper.

Dearest Megan,

If you're reading this letter it's because something happened to me and I'm not sitting there to grab it from your hands and pull it to pieces. (Admit it, you know I would, we would be struggling back and forth until I knocked you out of the chair and tickled you.) After all, I did tell you to wait till I got back to open the package. (I hope to God you are reading this.) I bought the ring from a little old lady at an open air market in Kabul. You would have been so captivated by this place, Megan, everything you could imagine from chickens, to fabric, to guns and jewelry, was being sold. Steps from guys like me and Taliban rebels hiding from each other. I paid a pretty penny for it too. But it's blue like the sky over Boston harbor. And the second I saw it, I knew it was meant for you. Just like I knew we were meant for each other. I wanted so badly to slip it on your finger and ask you to marry me. And that's what I'm doing right now. If there is an afterlife, I'm pushing against all the restraints to be there in front of you. I decided to mail it out, because I kept seeing this ghost. Or at least that's what I think he is. He calls himself the Shadow Soldier. I see him in my dreams, on patrol, in my waking hours, and even when we are in battles. Which there are way many more than you hear about on the news. We fight almost daily. I'm scared, Megan. He tells me to watch for the danger within, to prepare myself for the inevitable. Megan I feel like I'm going to die, and if I'm not going to die, than I must surely be going crazy. I miss you more than you will ever know. If something has happened to me, please go on and love again. I know that sounds like the bull shit you hear every guy say in every sappy movie.

But it's true. It's true. If you remember every Sunday afternoon that we had those two beers and a coke, and we toasted the memory of my Dad, sit another coke there for me. Keep living, keep loving, and keep going on.
All my love,
Bob

Megan folded the letter back up and choked on the sob in her throat. He had a feeling he was going to die. Maybe even had it before their last skype conversation. Oh my god, how scared he must have been. Tears were streaming down her face as she picked up the small velvet box and pushed back the lid. The sight of the ring made her gasp, covering her hand with her mouth she started to cry hysterically. The ring was stunning. One large blue stone reminiscent of a sapphire, surrounded by gold leaves, and perched atop a thin gold band. "Bob. Oh Bob, why can't you be here?" She snapped closed the lid of the box and kissed it before she closed it in the top drawer of her dresser, and crawled into her bed, with the letter clutched in her hand.

***

Megan snapped the cell phone up from the corner of her desk after the sixth ring. She had been back at work now for a few weeks, and everyone seemed to be giving her a wide berth. Her boss, who usually frowned upon personal calls, gave her a smile and turned the other way. Truth be told, the whole thing was starting to piss her off. She didn't expect the special treatment. She just wanted everyone to stop being so damn scared of making her sad. She had closed her feelings off after opening the ring, it was easier not to feel. Pretend it never existed. Still, she was snippy when she answered the call.

"Hello!"

Mitch wasn't expecting the snippy greeting. "Megan? It's Mitch, Mitch Crowley."

Megan bit back a snide 'I know who you are', and took in a deep breath. Shit. What could Mitch want? "Hi, Mitch. What's going on?"

"Well, I'm in Boston on leave, actually following up on a job offer for when I get out next year, and I didn't know if we could get together. I kind of have something I wanted to talk to you about." The tone of Mitch's voice changed, and Megan had a feeling she knew what he wanted to talk about. She had been seeing the strange man everywhere she went lately. Every bus stop and coffee shop. Every grocery store and restaurant. No matter where she was, the strange man dressed in fatigues would be in the shadows. And she would run from him, the more she tried to push Bob out of her mind and not feel, the more she saw him.

"Megan, are you there?"

"Yeah, I'm here, Mitch. I don't know what we could talk about, but I'm really busy putting this new program together and.."

Mitch cut her off mid-sentence. "I know you see him. I've been seeing him too, Megan. Everywhere I go, from the desert in Afghanistan to the terminal at Logan the other day, I see him. If you have seen him, the shadow soldier, I need to know. Please. I need to know I'm not crazy."

Megan clutched the phone tighter. "Temptations Café on Huntington Ave, meet me there at 7. I can't promise I have the answers, but I'll try." She hung up on him before she started to cry.

***

Mitch stood outside the small coffee house and laughed. When Megan had said Temptations café, his mind conjured up images of a strip club. So when the cab pulled up here, he breathed a sigh of relief. He hadn't relished the thought of meeting his buddies' girl at a dark hole in the wall. He pushed in to the brightly lit café and spotted Megan at the back. Sitting in one of the low booths, with her head in her hands and a steaming mug of coffee in front of her. She looked like hell. Nothing like the pictures plastered all over Bob's wall in the barracks, and even a little thinner and paler than she had at the funeral. A look he was sure was echoed in his own dark rimmed eyes. He cautiously approached her table.

"Megan?" She looked up and met his eyes with her own questioning ones.

"Mitch." Standing, she awkwardly held her hand out to him, and he surprised her by pulling her in for a hug.

"Are you okay?" Stumbling back from his grasp. She took him in. He looked tired and haggard. His hair that had once been shaggy like Bob's, was cut back to a military regulation haircut. His jeans and sweater hanging too big on his frame.

"Yah, I was just happy to see you. I'm glad you agreed to meet. Boston is an amazing city. I hope I get the job."

"What job did you apply for?"

Mitch laughed and waved the barista over for a coffee. "Head of security for the TSA at Logan."

Megan smiled weakly. "You certainly are qualified for that. I don't see why you wouldn't get it." She stopped and took a sip of her coffee. Over Mitch's left shoulder she made out the back of the stranger that had been haunting her. He was sitting at the counter. Nothing in front of him, and the other customers seemed to give him a wide berth. "He's here."

Her voice had been so quiet and small Mitch had barely heard her as he thanked the girl for his coffee. But the tired fear in her eyes gave him all the meaning he needed. "Who?" His voice came out just as small.

"Don't give me that, Mitch. On the phone you said it. The shadow soldier. The one following me since Bob died. You can see him, I can see him. Don't play coy with me." Tears threatened to spill over her lashes. Mitch instinctively reached for her hand and she swatted him away. "Not now. Tell me what you know."

Mitch sat back in the booth and sighed. "I saw him two days after Bob died, and almost daily since, no matter where I am. And then there was this." He reached into his pocket and took out the battered keychain and slid it across the table to Megan. "He gave it to me in Kabul. All I know is the name on his uniform was Clark. And I know that Bob never let that keychain out of his sight. It should have been on him when he died. There was no way in hell anyone else could have gotten it. Unless it fell out during the fire fight, but damn Megan, this guy wasn't even there that night. No one knows who the fuck he is. He doesn't exist."

Megan picked up the keychain and turned it over and over in her hands. She remembered the day they took that selfie. It was two days before Bob left for this last tour. One of the last times they had been together. Her heart broke again in a million pieces as she looked at it. All the feelings she was trying to bury since opening the package resurfacing again.

"Megan, I'm sorry. I failed Bob that night. I should have taken out every last rat bastard in that compound. I should have had his back. But he died a hero, Megan. He got that girl out, found her before any of us had a chance to secure the room."

Megan's head shot up. "What girl?"

Shit. Mitch had fucked up. Their mission had been top secret, no one was supposed to know about Delbar. Well, cat was out of the bag now. Mitch lowered his voice.

"That night we went into rescue a young girl from the Taliban. She was slated to be executed for helping US and ally troops across the Salang Pass. She also was teaching girls in her village to read, and to read in English. Bob found her before any of us and pulled her. He was wounded twice that night. His first hit was nothing, flesh wound, he killed the bastard that was ready to rape her. As we exited the compound one insurgent, I was going to let him live, his wife begged for him, grabbed a weapon and opened fire. Bob covered Delbar with his body and took a direct hit to the spinal column."

Megan was silently crying. Onlookers from close booths gave the couple privacy, but she still tried to hide her distress. This time she let Mitch take her hands.

"Megan. I'm sorry I failed him." Mitch was openly sobbing.

"No, Mitch! No, you did the right thing. You had no idea. It took amazing courage and humanity to give that man a second chance. You had no idea. It could have gone the other way. Bob knew what he was doing." Her voice lowered as she focused on the smiling faces on the key chain. "He knew what he was doing."

"But what about the shadow soldier? What does he want from us?" Mitch composed himself and took a long sip of his now tepid coffee.

"I don't know. But the more I try to push thoughts of Bob from my mind, the more I see him." Megan glanced to the counter as she spoke to see the man was no longer there. "He wants to tell us something. And I'm afraid whatever it is, it's bad. If soldiers only see this, Shadow Soldier, when they are going to die, then why are we seeing him?"

"I don't know." Mitch drained the last of his coffee. Looking at Megan's tired eyes, he felt a stirring deep down in his heart. She forgave him. He felt it in her touch, in her heat, in the way her eyes met his. She had set him free with her acceptance. Maybe they needed to set Bob free. Say goodbye through the Shadow Soldier. And god forgive him, he felt the need to love her. Was that too soon?

Staring deep in her eyes, fueled by her acceptance, he spoke. "I say the next time we see him, we confront him. Come on."

He rose from the booth and pulled Megan to her feet as he simultaneously threw five dollars on the table for their coffee. Holding her hand tightly, he walked from the coffee shop.

"Where are we going, Mitch?" She almost had a smile on her face, and felt hopeful for the first time in a month.

"To find Clark."

***

Walking through the crowded streets of the Fenway district, she realized she was taking comfort from Mitch's hand in hers. After they left the coffee shop they had hailed a cab for a few blocks east to Boston College, then they started to walk. Tempting fate. Walking, they traded tales about Bob in all walks of his life. Laughing at the silly things he did, and the way Mitch would go after him. Megan loved the stories from their time together in Ranger school, and could see how they had formed such a strong bond. And Mitch was delighted to finally have some light shed on the two beers and a coke story. And they both had tears in their eyes as they remembered his signature blend of tough devotion.

Sometime after three in the morning, they found themselves back on the steps of Megan's brownstone. Not ready to part ways from their shared awakening, but torn by the heat they were feeling. That's when Clark stepped from his shadow.

"Can you spare some change for an old veteran?"

"I don't know, buddy? Can you spare some intel?" Mitch's voice was cold.

"Depends by what you want for Intel." He eyed Megan as she tucked herself tighter around Mitch. "I trust you got your keychain back? Bob really wanted you to have it."

"I did. You've seen Bob." She stepped away from Mitch, a tad embarrassed to be seen so close to him.

"You didn't have to move." The shadow grew brighter as he talked. "Bob told you he wanted you to go on. And Mitch, he's an honest man, a devoted soldier. He doesn't blame you for that night." The soldier bore his eyes into Mitch. "He wants you to take care of her."

"Why can't we see him? Why did he send you?" Megan's voice grew distressed.

"Just the way it has to be. You're both fighting battles of your own. You can either continue how you have been, and I'll come for you soon. Or, you can heal, move on. Bob has another mission. He's just regrouping, you can call it that I guess."

Mitch reached out and his hand passed through the soldier, like nothing was there. "Can you tell him something for us?"

The shadow grew faint as the soldier nodded. "It is allowed."

"Tell him we're sorry."

The shadow shook as the soldier laughed. "He doesn't need the forgiveness of man where he is. But he needs you to forgive yourselves, no matter what happens next."

With that the man was gone, a cloud of vapor hanging in his place.

"What the hell does that mean? No matter what happens next."

The only answer he received was Megan pulling him in for a deep kiss.

"I have no idea."

The End

Bonus Content

Panel 35

Twilight was fast approaching, the sun setting in soft pinks and yellows on the other side of the Potomac. From her vantage point on the steps of the Lincoln Memorial, Rachel could see all the way from one side of the mall to the other. The view was familiar, the bridges and parkways behind her leading back into Virginia. Blossoming cherry trees were on her left and right, their soft pink reassuring her as they lazily swayed in the late April breeze. And, of course, the black granite wall to her left rose and faded with the knoll. She watched as the last of the tourists made their way down its length, laughing and posing for pictures, tossing roses and scraps of paper at its base. When she was sure she wouldn't be interrupted, she rose from her step and made her way down and across the road, side stepping a couple who lazily walked with their arms around each other, and nodded at the peddler pushing his cart of gaudy, overpriced souvenirs.

Then she was there, standing face to face with the cold granite, embroidered with the names of people once alive, once loved, who once breathed and fought for her, and her country, with everything they had. She started to walk the length of it, her left hand tracing circles on the granite until it disappeared into the ground, her right hand holding the dangling dog tags that tinkled and chimed. She turned and retraced her steps, heading back toward Lincoln as he watched her solemn procession, never paying attention to the growing darkness or the chill the air was taking.

Until he spoke. "Miss? Excuse me Miss. Do you think it's wise to be out here after dark all alone? I mean, you do know that DC has one hell of a crime rate."

She turned to see a soldier standing there, his dress uniform pressed and neat, but bearing the effects of a long day in the early spring heat of the south. He looked tired and weary, but she didn't feel threatened by him. Something in his eyes told her he was safe.

"Thanks for your concern, but I am meeting my father here. We meet here every year at this time. It's kind of our thing. He should be here soon." She twisted the dog tags a little tighter in her hand, pushing her own damp hair off her face.

The soldier looked around at the rapidly emptying park and nodded. "Does your father live in DC?"

Rachel shook her head. "No, well not really, he doesn't really live anywhere. So you could say he does. Do you?"

The soldier shook his head. "No ma'am. I was over in Arlington. Umm we laid one of our guys to rest today. A lot of the guys went drinking, but I had never been here before and wanted to see the memorials before I headed back to Dover."

Rachel eyed him. "I'm sorry for your loss. It must be hard. I know how standing there feels. But Dover? You're not wearing an Air Force uniform."

The soldier chuckled, the sound not reaching his eyes. "No mam I'm not. Joint endeavor right now, I'm stationed there temporarily with the MP force before I cycle out. I'm taking early retirement. You have family in Arlington?"

She shook her head and averted her eyes back toward the Washington Monument. "No, I just know how it is to be at a military funeral. I'm driving back to Mass tomorrow. I'm sorry for prying. And like I said, I'm sorry you lost one of your guys."

With that she turned to make her way back down the wall, continuing her silent vigil. But something in her eyes unsettled the soldier. He was worried about her. He stood where he was and waited for her to turn and make her way back.

"Oh, you're still here."

The soldier chuckled. "Yes, Ma'am, I just don't feel right leaving you here. It's just about dark. If you want, I can call my superior and he will vouch for me. But let me wait with you."

Rachel eyed him a minute. He was handsome and strong. She could see that much in the fading light. He was also war weary. She had seen that look on other soldiers back from deployment. But something in his eyes made her trust him. The deep, icy blue reminded her of her dad's. "Okay. But you have to call me Rachel instead of Ma'am'. Okay? And I'm scared he won't come if he sees you with me. He's very shy, and already an hour late."

The soldier extended his hand. "Okay, Rachel. I'm Sergeant Blake Kawoski. But you can call me Blake." He winked, which made her blush as she took his hand to shake it. "If your dad is that late do you want to try and call him?"

Rachel pulled her hand back. "No, I can't call him. He doesn't have a cell phone. I just have to trust he will be here. Every year on this date he meets me here."

Panic was starting to edge into her voice and Blake saw the tears building in her eyes. If the bastard didn't show he would hunt him down and have a bone to pick with him. He was already feeling possessive toward the petite girl in front of him. Her dark hair and green eyes made her pale peaches and cream complexion stand out. She talked like she was educated. She dressed like she was a country girl. He felt like taking her for coffee and trying to figure her out. He was so glad he came to the wall instead of to a bar with the guys. He felt like he was here for a reason.

"Well, Rachel, do you want to go sit on one of the benches by the reflecting pool? I'm sure we could see him come from there."

She shook her head, getting visibly agitated. "No. I have to stay right here. He always meets me at panel 35. If I move, he won't know where to find me."

A tear fell down her cheek. It struck deep into Blake's heart and he reached out to wipe it away. Something was wrong here. And he needed to get to the bottom of it.

"Okay. Well, we are in front of 35 so why don't we sit here?" Blake looked at her with a sad smile and sat down on the ground, folding his legs into a position like he was going to meditate.

Rachel stood there staring at him for a second, 'til he laughed and patted the ground. "Come on, I saved the best seat for you."

Besides her panicked state, she had to admit it was better to have someone to wait with. She sat down, careful to leave a few inches of space between them, all the while wondering if Blake thought she was some kind of lunatic. She had to admit, waiting around the Memorial at night alone was not always the smartest thing. Every year she made her friend promise to stay home, over the bridge in Herndon, and wait for her. In the ten years she had been doing this she had never gotten into trouble. But her dad had never been late either. She stole a sideways glance at Blake and he was watching her. She blushed and dipped her head.

"So Rachel, you say you're from Massachusetts. I grew up in Nashua, New Hampshire, but my grandmother lived in Sturbridge. So I'm pretty familiar with central Mass."

She smiled a big smile that he wanted her to keep on her face forever. "Really? I'm from Worcester, Mass. Small world. I guess you are all right."

Blake laughed again, a sound she wouldn't mind hearing forever. The thought made Rachel blush as he continued to talk. "Yah, we always say it is. Are those your dad's dog tags? I'm assuming he served in Vietnam from where we are sitting."

"Yah, they are." She hadn't realized she had started playing with the dog tags, wrapping them back and forth between her fingers, taking comfort in the cool metal. "He served in the 25th Infantry Division during the Tet Offensive."

Blake looked at her. "No shit? I was stationed for a time with the 25th in Hawaii. In-between tours in Afghanistan. He must have been bad-ass, to survive the offensive. I had a drill sergeant in Basic who did. Lost a shit ton of buddies though."

Rachel nodded. She was so afraid her dad wasn't going to come with Blake sitting next to her. But she also wanted to know more about him. She inched closer, their legs now touching as the night grew colder.

"He was wounded there. Screwed out of his Purple Heart, like so many of his guys. But hey, you must be bad-ass too. All those tours in Afghanistan." She tried to switch the conversation away from her Dad. She didn't like to share him.

"I like to say stupid. This last was my last one. I'm out in six months. Laying Bob to rest was the worst thing I ever had to do. I thought we would make it through, our unit, never losing a guy. Than that last one, shit." He looked down and shook his head.

The night grew quiet around them and she saw his shoulders shake. Inching closer, she laid a hand on his back and put her head on his. They sat that way for a while, quiet and contemplative, 'til Blake raised his head and looked at her. "At least I was scheduled to get out before all that. Damn. Wouldn't want anyone to say I was a quitter."

She looked at him, her own tears wetting her eyes. "I couldn't ever see someone mistaking you for a quitter."

Blake nodded. "Thanks. I feel like I have known you forever, Rachel."

All of a sudden, they were both aware of a man standing in front of them. He was older, small in stature, wearing jeans and cowboy boots, and a pair of glasses that looked straight out of the seventies. He smiled, and Rachel shot up off the ground faster than Blake thought humanly possible. "Daddy!!!!" She threw herself in his arms, dropping the dog tags. Blake reached out and picked them up before he stood up himself. "Daddy, I told Blake you would be here. Oh, I hope you don't mind he waited with me."

The man looked Blake up and down before he extended his hand. "Not at all, baby. Thanks for waiting with my girl. Name's Wayne. And you are?"

Blake took the man's hand. His was cold, even though the night was comfortable. "Sergeant Blake Kawoski. Nice to meet you, sir."

"Ahh, are you active duty, son?"

Blake shook his head. "Not much longer, sir. I'm being discharged in six months. Early retirement."

The older man looked away from Blake and at his daughter. "Smart man, Blake. The way things are going, you're making the right choice. Damn shame what they have you guys into. It's like this hell hole all over again." He gestured toward the Wall.

"Yes sir. Well, I will leave you two to your visit and get going. Thank you for the pleasure of waiting with you, Rachel." Blake nodded his head and turned to go, when Wayne stopped him.

"Son, if you don't mind, could you wait here for Rachel and walk her back to her car when we are done? I hate the thought of her being out here all alone."

"I can do that, sir. If it's all right with Rachel." Something told Blake that her independent nature wouldn't go for it.

"Really, Dad, Blake doesn't have to wait for me. All these years I have done it myself. I'm sure the sergeant has better stuff to do."

But when Rachel looked at Blake, her eyes told a different story. They were begging him to stay.

He wanted to. He wanted more time with this girl. "Rachel, go with your dad, I'll sit right here, panel 35, and wait. Seriously, I have nothing better to do." Blake sat back down on the ground and folded his arms over his chest.

Wayne laughed. "Well, Sweetie Pie, I think Blake has made up your mind for you. Let's go for a stroll."

Wayne winked at Blake and turned to go walk to the west end of the wall, his arm linked with Rachel's, who was now looking at Blake with an apologetic face. Blake could only laugh. As he watched them walk away it struck him that he had seen Wayne somewhere before. Like this morning at Bob's service at Arlington. Was he a family member? A random passerby? He looked at the two as they sat on a bench. Rachel was talking really fast, her head on her dad's shoulder like it had been on his earlier. It struck him just how intimate a gesture that must be for her, and it warmed him head to toe. He would wait here all night for her if he had to.

Sometime later, they walked back up to the 35th panel from the west, the one where Blake was now leaning against and fiddling with his I-phone. Rachel had wet eyes, but a wide smile. As Blake jumped up to greet them, he noticed a cold wind rush past, but the tree branches didn't even stir. Rachel shuddered and stepped closer to Blake.

"My daughter here tells me that you lost a man. I'm sorry, son. Just please don't stop living, don't hide from the world. That's no way to honor his memory at all. What you have seen may have scared you, but don't let it define you. Show your scares with pride."

Blake nodded at the older man. "Yes, sir. You may have known him. I could have sworn I saw you at Arlington earlier today."

Wayne shifted uncomfortably. "Well, I have been doing some work over there. Consulting you can call it. But I don't think I knew him personally."

Blake took Rachel's hand without really thinking, but she surprised him by entwining her fingers with his. "I was thinking, maybe I could take you both for a late dinner. I don't know DC at all, but I'm sure we can find a quiet restaurant."

Rachel spoke up. "Dad has to go. I'm not sure if I should impose on you like that."

"Oh, go with the young man, Rachel. Don't worry about me. I know people, and this one, this one you should hold onto. He has a soul unlike any I have seen."

Blake looked between the two, and felt a strange pull back from the wall. He stepped toward the sidewalk, pulling Rachel with him, just as Wayne stepped into the shadow of the granite panel.

"Dad isn't coming back again." Her statement was resolute and quiet as tears streamed down her face. "He can't. I won't see him again."

"Why? Wayne, there isn't any way you can see Rachel again? Are you okay?"

Wayne chuckled and seemed to grow fainter in the dark. Blake rubbed at his eyes. "She won't need me anymore son. And I have other places I'm needed. But, I'll always be here."

He reached behind him and patted the granite, a soft light emitting from his hand where it made contact. "Take care of her for me, Sergeant. That's an order."

Right after he said it, Wayne stepped forward and into the
dark abyss of panel 35, disappearing before their eyes. As he did,
Blake let go of Rachel's hand and stepped forward. What the hell
had he just seen? Blake touched the panel and felt nothing but the
cool granite and the etched names, rough under his fingertips.
Turning back toward Rachel, he saw her standing there with tears
cascading down her face. "Rachel, what the hell just happened?"

Rachel jumped at the sound of his voice. "He always does
that. I only get an hour with him each year and then he's gone.
Now he won't be back again. He's a ghost Blake." She leaned
into Blake's chest and sobbed. "I have never told anyone because
they might think I'm crazy. But now you saw it, a stranger. I
understand if you want to run from this spot."

Blake held her at arm's length and took in her pained face.
"I'm not going anywhere, sweetie." He turned and took her by
the hand over to the wall. Running his hand up and down the
length of the panel, he saw faces looking back at him. Slowly
walking the length of the west end of the wall, he continued to
see images, men in varying uniforms and conditions, all smiling
at him and some saluting. When they got to the end where the
wall disappeared into the ground, he heard taps play in the
distance, and saw blue wisps of smoky forms descending.

"I'll be damned. In Afghanistan we told tales of old soldiers
seen in the field after an attack, someone we had never seen
before who would be gone when the smoke cleared. Bob said
they were spirits of the fallen welcoming home the lost. Bob was,
he was out there, and we never paid attention to him. But this
morning, over in Arlington, I could have sworn I saw your father.
It hit me after we had been talking for a while. He was there,
walking slowly from the gravesite." Blake stopped and ran his
fingers through his thick hair. "Shit. I wouldn't have believed it if
I hadn't seen it. But why? You said your dad came home? Why is
he here?"

"He did. He passed twenty years later from cancer. Cancer
everyone was convinced was brought on by his exposure to
Agent Orange. He was never right Blake. He was lost from the
second he got back on American soil, robbed of his purple heart,

forgotten. I'd rather remember him as the ghost he has been the last ten years. He seems to have found his place, his mission. We have never been closer than this one day a year." She stopped and stifled a sob. "Now he says he won't be back. That he compelled you to come here so we could meet."

"Holy shit, Rachel." Blake sank to the ground and dragged Rachel to his lap. Coincidence? Maybe. He could have just as easily gone with the guys drinking instead of coming to the Wall. But after seeing the old man walk silently from Arlington earlier, he felt like he needed to pay respects here. He never thought he would be face to face with the hundreds of souls he had just seen, or the beautiful girl in his arms. "How did you find him?"

"It was chance. I came down here ten years ago to see my best friend. Her husband works at the Pentagon. We were exploring the city one night, two young girls fresh out of college. I made her take me here, Dad had never gotten to see it. Next thing I know, she is over talking with some girl from their condo, and a hand rests on my shoulder. I turn, and it's my dad. Took me a long time to accept it, Blake. I came down here the same time the next year, and he's always here April 11th, at dusk."

Blake stood and slowly pulled Rachel to her feet. Taking her by the hand, he wiped the last tears from her cheeks. "Can I take you for the late dinner now?" She nodded and pulled him closer. Walking back toward the Lincoln Memorial, they briefly stopped in front of Panel 35. Blake let go of Rachel's hand and stood at attention, saluting the fallen, saluting Wayne. The reflection thrown back at him in the polished granite wasn't his own. It was Wayne's, saluting him.

One year later:

The couple stood at the top of the Lincoln memorial waiting for the last of the tourists to leave. Blake knew the park rangers would be asking people to leave tonight. They were making a sweep to pick up mementos and clean the grounds. But he had to show Rachel something. When it was finally deserted, except for a few soldiers, he took her hand and led her down the stairs and across the road.

"Do you have our wedding picture, sweetie?"

She nodded. "Yes, but I don't know why we are leaving it there. Dad's not on there. I don't even know if he's in there anymore."

Blake just smiled. "Let's go see."

They walked hand in hand down the Wall until they found panel 35. Easy enough for all the time they had spent there. When they stopped, Blake knelt down and reached for Rachel's hand. "Take a look, Hun."

Rachel knelt down and looked where Blake was pointing. At the bottom of the panel in freshly carved letters was her dad's name. Wayne Williams. "But how? How Blake?" Tears were streaming down Rachel's face.

"I pulled some strings and found some records. Got some things declassified, and petitioned for his name to be added. Usually it takes years, can be done but it's hard. Pays to know people." Rachel stared in disbelief as Blake took the wedding picture from her hand and placed it at the base of panel 35. "Now we know he will always be here."

As they knelt there in the setting sun, the face of her father looked back at them, surrounded by the faces of countless other men who deserved to be remembered. Blake stood and saluted.

The End

Author's Note

Thank you for purchasing and reading this second edition of The Shadow Soldier. It contains new content, an expanded beginning of how Megan and Bob met, as well as the bonus short story, Panel 35, which has never been in print before.

All three stories have connecting characters. And Panel 35 expands on the Shadow Soldier. In fact, all of these stories hold a special place in my heart. Through them I hope the memories of my dad, and a young soldier special to my family, live on. So as always a large portion of the proceeds of this book will be donated to the Wounded Warrior Project in the memory of Pfc. Keely Walsh.

No soldier should be forgotten. Whether they died in combat, or on American soil. They have given of their time and life for this country. We are no doubt a country in turmoil, not perfect by any means, but we still are America. We are still forged in unity and patriotism. And I can think of no place I would rather live, and I will continue to support our United States Military.

Please visit the Wounded Warrior website at
http://www.woundedwarriorproject.org/

About The Author

Becca Boucher was born and raised in Worcester Massachusetts. Her father instilled an early love of reading and encouraged her when she started to write. Rebecca earned a degree in Criminal Justice from Quinsigamond Community College, but her love has always been writing.

After the birth of her first child, she moved to a quiet little town on the edge of Worcester County, in the heart of Central Massachusetts. Living there has inspired her to write most of her current projects. In fact, local readers might recognize some of her locations. Currently, Rebecca is a freelance writer and blogger. Her first novel, Hunting The Moon (The Moon Series) debuted December 2013 from Write More Publications. Followed by the second book in the series, Midnight Raven. She has also authored three short stories and one novella, The Shadow Soldier.

When she is not writing, Rebecca is the mother to two boys, ages 12 and 15. Two of Rebecca's favorite causes are Autism Awareness and Veteran's causes. All proceeds of her book, The Shadow Soldier, have been donated to the Wounded Warrior Project.

Find Becca on Amazon at:
http://www.amazon.com/s/ref=dp_byline_sr_ebooks_1?ie=U
TF8&text=Becca+Boucher&search-alias=digital-text&field-
author=Becca+Boucher&sort=relevancerank

Made in the USA
Charleston, SC
10 November 2015